EARLY MORNING
IN THE BARN

NANCY TAFURI

GREENWILLOW BOOKS·NEW YORK

permission in writing from the
Publisher, Greenwillow Books,
a division of William Morrow
& Company, Inc., 105 Madison
Avenue, New York, N.Y. 10016.
Printed in U.S.A.   First Edition
8 7 6 5 4 3 2 1

Library of Congress Cataloging in Publication Data
Tafuri, Nancy.   Early morning in the barn.
Summary: All the barnyard animals wake up when
the rooster crows.   [1. Stories without words.
2. Domestic animals — Pictorial works] I. Title.
PZ7.T117Ear 1983   [E]   83-1436
ISBN 0-688-02328-2   ISBN 0-688-02329-0 (lib. bdg.)

FOR TOM *Thank You*

Cock
a
doodle
doo

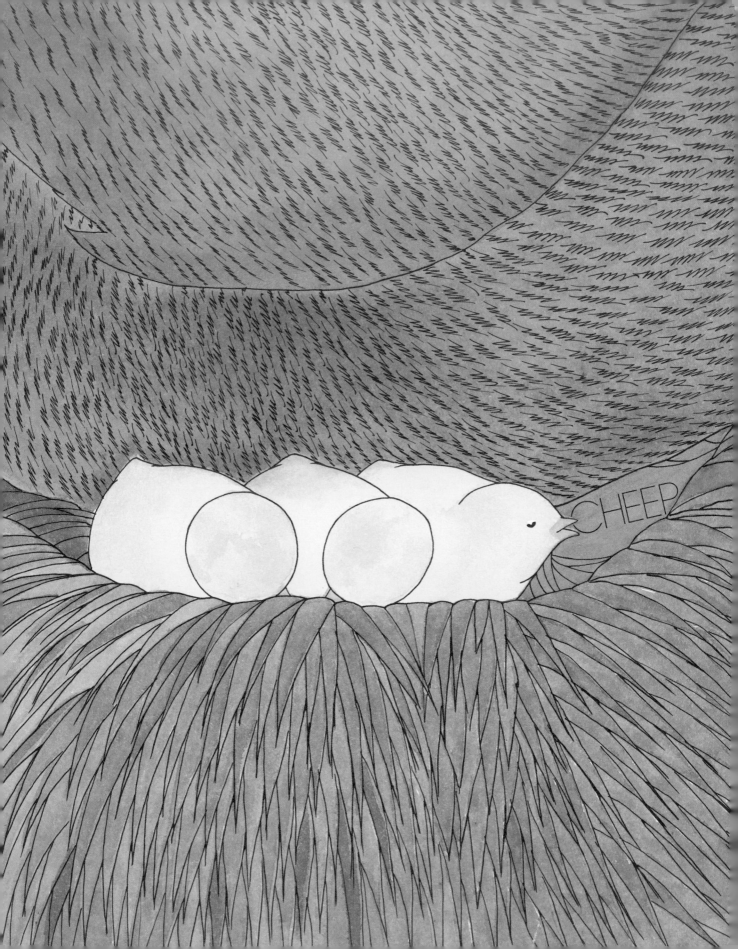

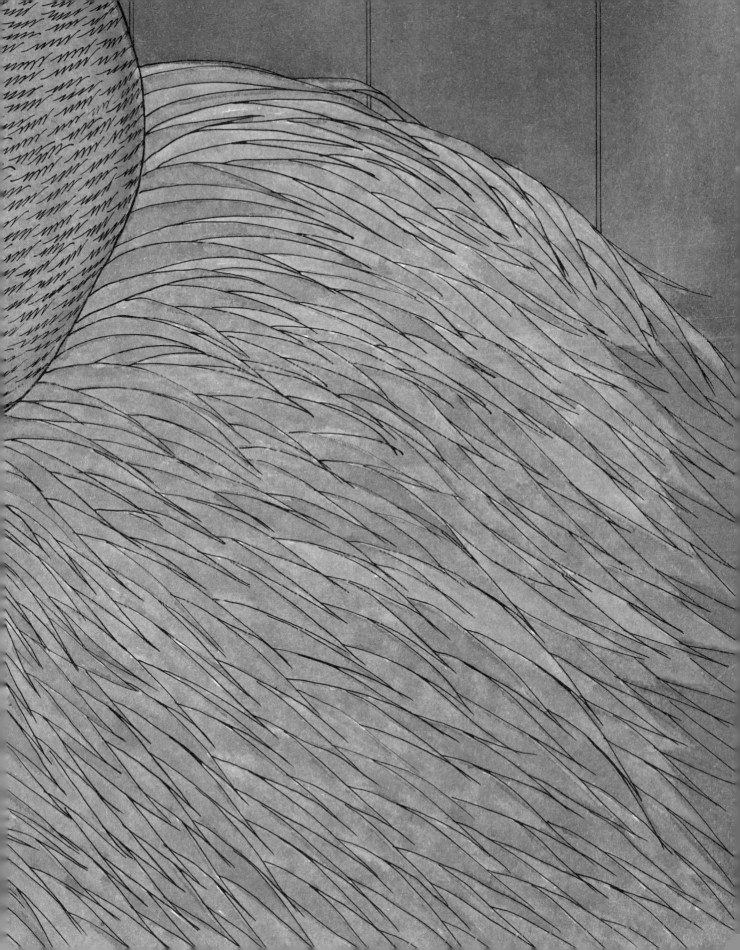

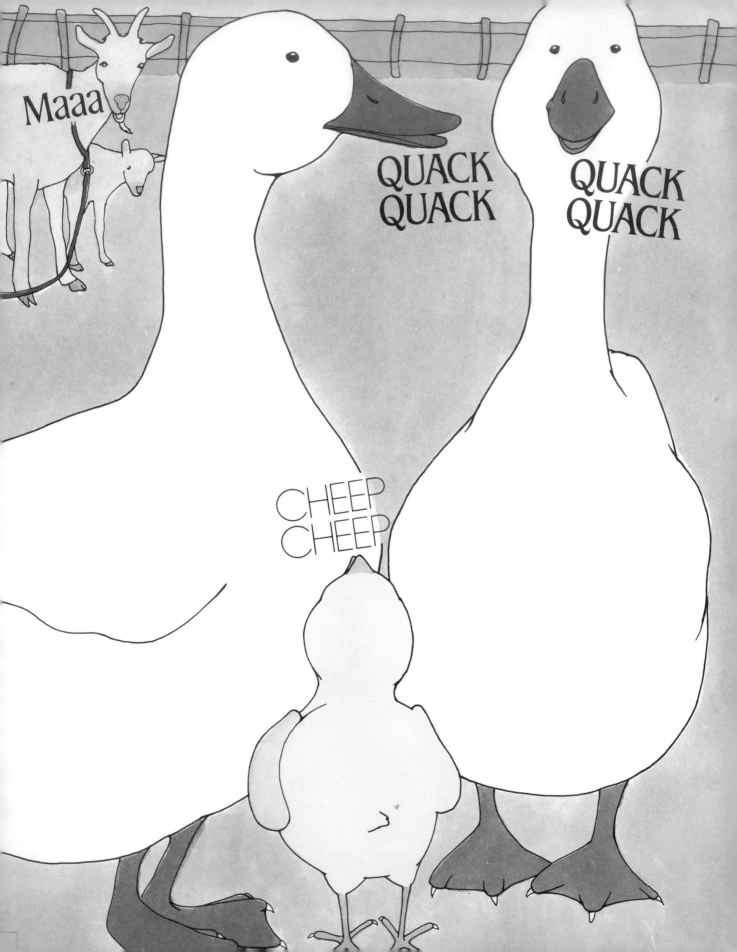

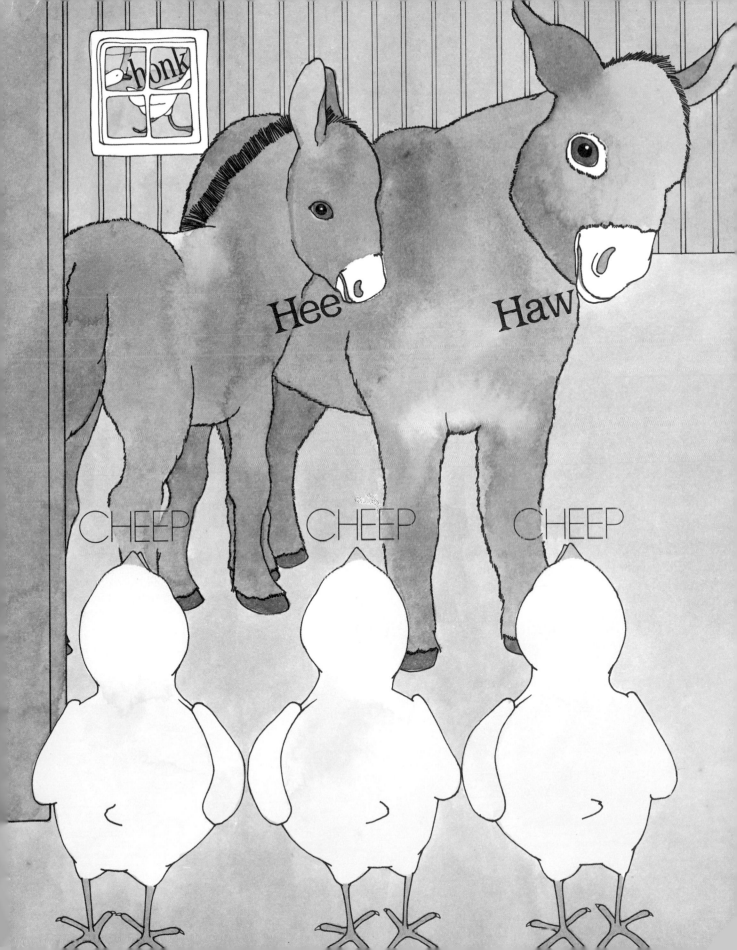

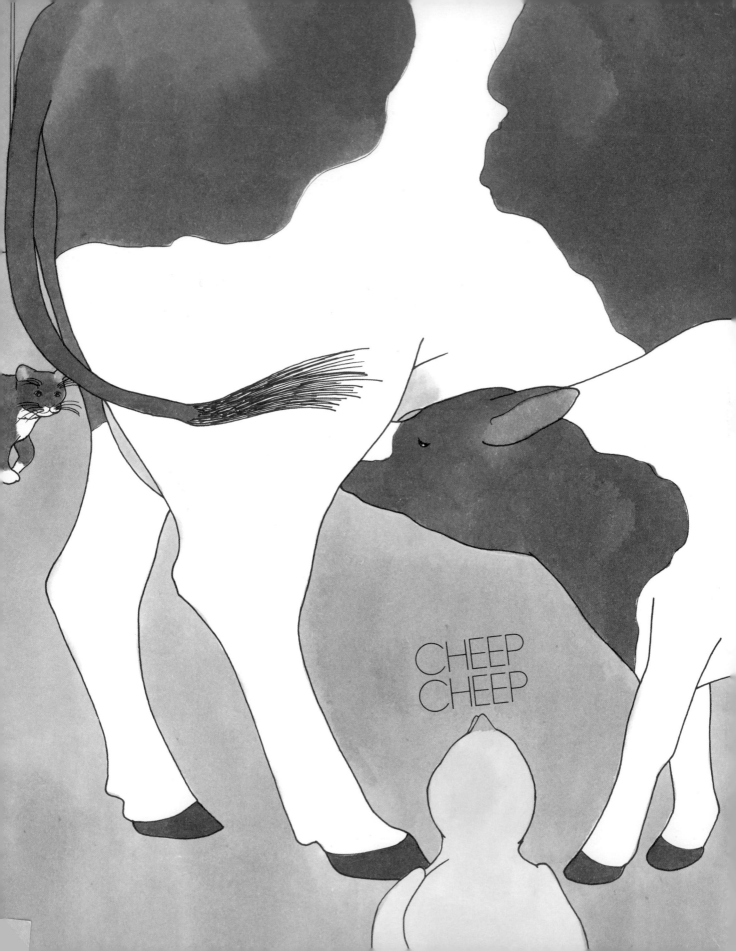